FUN TIME

WITH THE ALPHABET

BY

Felix "CHINOMALO" Robles

To order additional copies of this book, contact:
Xlibris
844-714-8691
www.Xlibris.com
Orders@Xlibris.com

ISBN: Softcover   978-1-6641-3072-2
        EBook   978-1-6641-3071-5

Print information available on the last page

Rev. date: 09/26/2020

Fun Time

with the alphabet

School is out for Summer,and the letters A thru
Z can't wait to start having fun

A and B went fishing.

C and D want to ride bike.

E,F and G are all riding skateboard.

While H and I went to the pool.

J,K and L love to play soccer.

M,N and O decide to go on a boat ride in a small Pond.

While P,Q and R play baseball.

And S,T and U have a Gokart and ride it down a safe hill

V and W go fly kites together.

XY and Z decided to go out to the park and play on the slide

Printed in the United States
By Bookmasters